This book belongs to:

_____

Huggy Buggy

by Leslie Eagle

illustrated by Lynne Jones

To my first huggy buggies –
Brook and Jessica

Leslie Eagle

To my beloved grandchildren

Lynne Jones

Find the matching little bugs near
Huggy Buggy throughout the book.

Huggy Buggy little one,
loving you is so much fun!

Huggy Buggy silly one,

Twirling round and round

Huggy Buggy silly one,
tumbling to the ground

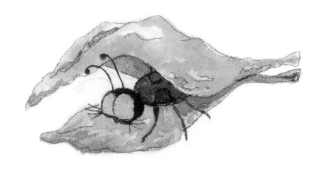

Huggy Buggy happy one,
hiding all around

Huggy Buggy happy one,
running to be found

Huggy Buggy quiet one,
tiptoe up and down

Huggy Buggy quiet one,
do not make a sound

Huggy Buggy sleepy one,
slowly settle down

Huggy Buggy sleepy one,
happy dreams be found

Huggy Buggy little one,
Loving you is so much fun!